SAM SILVER: UNDERCOVER PIRATE

KIDNAPPED

Collect all the Sam Silver: Undercover Pirate *books*

KIDNAPPED

Jan Burchett and Sara Vogler

Illustrated by Leo Hartas

Orion
Children's Books

First published in Great Britain in 2012
by Orion Children's Books
a division of the Orion Publishing Group Ltd
Orion House
5 Upper St Martin's Lane
London WC2H 9EA
An Hachette UK company

1 3 5 7 9 10 8 6 4 2

Text copyright © Jan Burchett and Sara Vogler 2012
Map and interior illustrations copyright © Leo Hartas 2012

The right of Jan Burchett and Sara Vogler to be identified
as the authors of this work and the right of Leo Hartas to be
identified as the illustrator of this work have been asserted.

The Orion Publishing Group's policy is to use papers that are natural,
renewable and recyclable products and made from wood grown in sustainable
forests. The logging and manufacturing processes are expected to conform to
the environmental regulations of the country of origin.

A catalogue record for this book is
available from the British Library.

ISBN 978 1 4440 0586 8

Printed in Great Britain by Clays Ltd, St Ives plc

For Leo Dyche,
and in memory of Zachary.

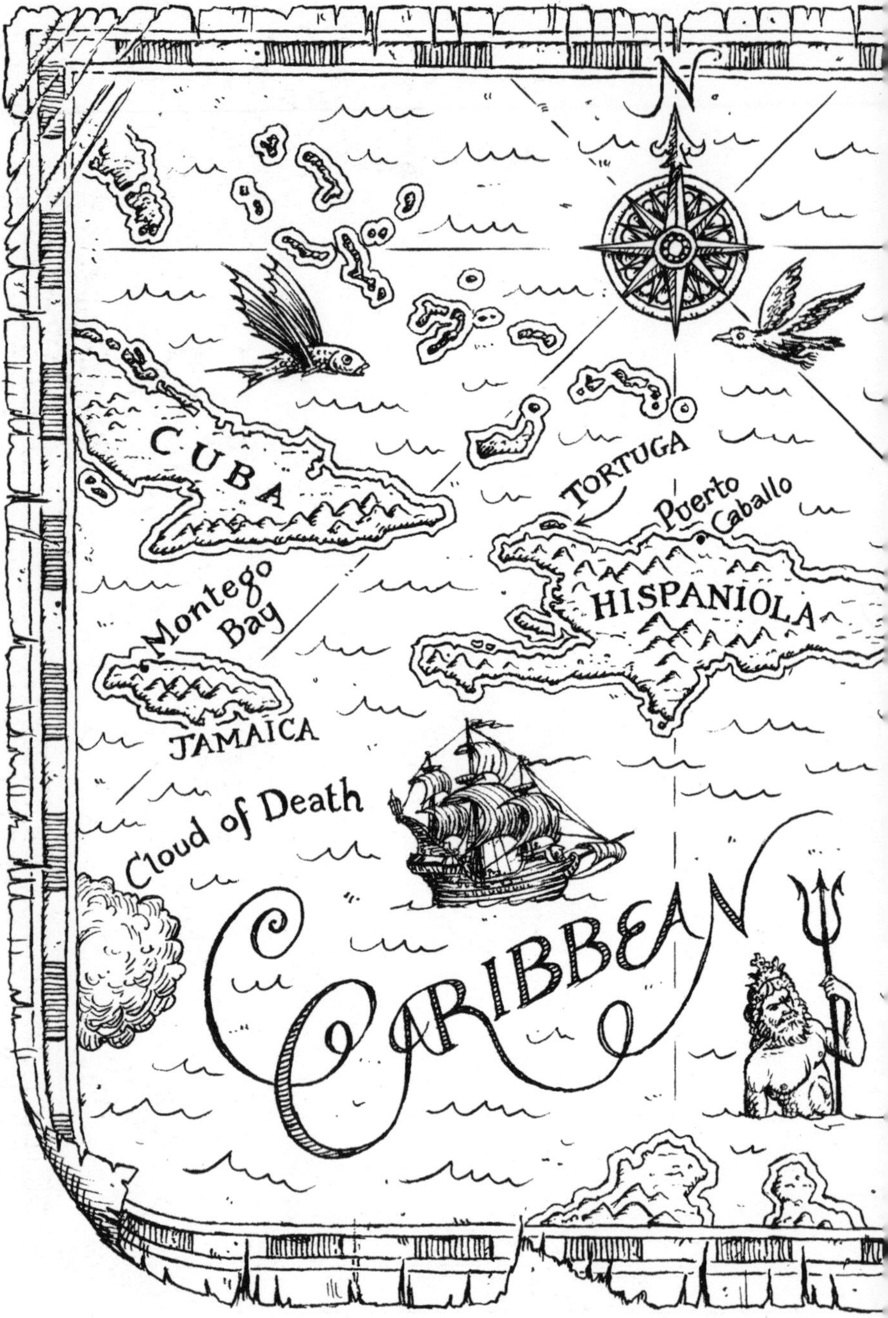

N
CUBA
TORTUGA
Puerto Caballo
HISPANIOLA
Montego Bay
JAMAICA
Cloud of Death
CARIBBEAN

COLONIES
OF THE
NEW
WORLD

Here be Treasure

SKELETON ISLAND

Gibbet Point

DRAGON ISLAND

Bridgetown
BARBADOS

S E A

The
SEA
WOLF

Captain's
Cabin
Hammocks
Gun Deck
Galley
Ship's Stores

CHAPTER ONE

Sam Silver picked up his football and raced out of his bedroom. He was off to the beach for an important match with his friends and there wasn't a minute to spare. He made for the stairs that led from the flat to his parents' fish and chip shop below.

Thump! He collided with something solid that grunted.

It was his dad.

"Watch it, Sam!" said his father, staggering back on to the dirty-washing basket. "Why are you in your football kit? Hurry up and change. Arnold will be here in a minute."

Sam nearly dropped his football in horror. He'd forgotten all about Arnold. His mother's cousin was the most boring person in the whole world, if not in the whole universe. Mum always made him dress up in his smartest clothes when Arnold visited and it was impossible to sit still and listen while Arnold droned on and on.

"I have to go down to the beach," he protested. "I've got a really important game with my mates."

"You can't play football when Arnold's coming," insisted his dad. "You know he'll be upset if you're not here. Now get changed."

Sam mooched back into his bedroom and pulled out his best shirt and trousers. He wondered what Cousin Arnold would lecture them about this time. Bee-keeping in Tudor England? Which toothpicks the ancient Egyptians used? Knitting in the Middle Ages? Arnold knew loads about history and managed to make it all sound really boring.

Well, Sam knew something Arnold didn't know. He knew how it felt to travel back three hundred years in time to a pirate ship in the Caribbean and have awesome adventures. It was Sam's big secret. One day he'd found an old glass bottle, washed up on the beach of his home in Backwater Bay. Inside was a gold coin sent by Joseph Silver, Sam's pirate ancestor. It had been filthy so he'd tried to clean it with a bit of spit and a rub. The next thing he knew he'd found himself aboard a real pirate ship, the *Sea Wolf*, with Captain Blade and his band of fearsome buccaneers.

Sam tried to imagine Arnold on board the *Sea Wolf*. It would be a disaster. Arnold would bore the crew so much they'd all be fighting to walk the plank after five minutes!

An idea suddenly catapulted into Sam's brain. Arnold might not be welcome on the pirate ship — but Sam knew the crew would be delighted to see *him*! And, as no time ever passed when he slipped off to the Caribbean, he could have a swashbuckling adventure and still be back in time for Arnold's visit.

Sam threw down his smart clothes and quickly put on the scruffy T-shirt, jeans and trainers he always wore for his time travelling. He couldn't risk coming back from an adventure with his best shirt and trousers dirty and ripped.

He carefully took the bottle from the collection of beach treasures displayed on his shelf and shook out the gold coin. He spat on the doubloon – Silver Spit seemed to be the magic ingredient – and rubbed it on his sleeve.

"*Sea Wolf*, here I come!" he yelled.

There was a loud rushing sound and Sam felt as if he were caught in a whirlwind. The furniture set off in a wild spin round his head. Sam closed his eyes tightly. He didn't want to get time-travel sickness. When the spinning stopped he felt himself land on a hard wooden floor. He could smell rope and tar and hot, salty air. He opened his eyes. Great! He was back in the little storeroom on the *Sea Wolf*. He rammed his coin deep in his back pocket.

A tatty jerkin, belt and a spyglass – an old-fashioned telescope – lay in a heap on a barrel. His friend, Charlie, must have put them there, ready for his next appearance. She was the only one who knew his time-travelling secret.

A black cat was curled up on top of the pile. It opened one eye and gave him an evil stare.

"Good boy, Sinbad," Sam said nervously, trying to edge forward.

Merow! A set of vicious claws flashed out. Sam leapt back.

Sinbad, the ship's cat, was fiercely loyal to the crew. And fierce was the word. None of the pirates dared go near him

except for Charlie. The mangy cat adored her and turned into a purring ball of fur whenever she was near.

Sinbad arched his back, gave a hiss and leapt out of the door.

Before the cat could change his mind, Sam quickly put on the jerkin and belt and grabbed his spyglass.

Now he was ready for action!

CHAPTER TWO

Sam raced up the steep wooden steps to the deck, and blinked in the dazzling sunlight. The ship was out in the middle of the blue ocean. A brisk wind filled the dirty, patched sails and made the flag at the top of the mainmast flap wildly. The flag, with its snarling wolf's head above the crossed bones, looked fierce enough to scare the toughest enemy. So did the captain. Captain Blade stood at the wheel, weapons gleaming in the belts across his chest as he shouted orders to the men in the rigging.

Sam could hear the chink of coins. A horde of pirates was jostling round a large casket. His friend, Fernando, was scooping out doubloons into a sack, his curly hair bursting out from the bandana tied round his head. Sam crept up behind him.

"Avast!" he whispered in his best pirate voice. "I'll have that gold before you can say cat-o-nine-tails!"

Fernando swung round, ready for a fight, and his face broke into a wide grin. "Look who's turned up," he called in his strong Spanish accent. "It's Sam Silver."

The pirates gave a rousing cheer and the captain raised his tricorn hat in welcome, keeping his station at the wheel.

"Well, polish me spyglass with a sea

sponge!" cried Ned. The bosun had a
beaming smile on his plump face. "Good
to see you, Sam. Been to visit your mum?
She's lucky to have a dutiful son like
you."

All pirates loved their mothers, so
Charlie had come up with this excuse to
explain why Sam disappeared every now
and then. It was true because he *was* going
home to his mum – and it was much easier

than trying to explain about the three-hundred-year time difference!

"Stap me vitals!" exclaimed Harry Hopp, the first mate. "You're back just in time to see our magnificent haul. We stole it from the *Lucky Gull*." He tapped the casket with his wooden leg.

"Not so lucky for them," added Ned happily. "Though those scurvy knaves made a good fight of it." The pirates let out a hearty laugh and gave each other playful punches on their tattooed arms.

"Awesome!" gasped Sam. He realised Harry and Ned were looking at him strangely. *Whoops!* he thought. *Pirates from 1706 won't understand what awesome means.* "Er . . . I mean, we can buy oars . . . some new oars with that."

"We don't need new oars," said Harry Hopp, scratching his bald head. "We need food and weapons."

"Sam!" Charlie came running up the

steps from the gun deck. She slapped Sam on the back, sending him staggering. Charlotte Fleetwood was an orphan, with a lot of money and an evil stepfather who wanted to get his hands on it. She'd decided that she'd be safer on a pirate ship than anywhere near him. With her hair roughly chopped and her ragged breeches she looked like a real boy pirate.

Captain Blade handed the wheel over to Harry Hopp and strode across the deck. "Pleased to have you back on board, lad."

"Do you want me on lookout, Captain?" asked Sam.

"Aye," said the captain. "We're off to Tortuga to spend our treasure and we don't want anyone creeping up to steal it from us. Keep a weather eye out for enemies."

Sam made for the rigging, stepping over the casket and bags of doubloons. He'd just climbed into the wooden crow's nest

at the top of
the main mast
when something
heavy landed on his
head with a loud squawk.
A feathered head bent
down and peered at him with
piercing black eyes.

It was the *Sea Wolf* parrot.

"Ahoy there, me hearty!" he squawked in Sam's ear.

"Ahoy there, Crow!" exclaimed Sam. "Hope you've been keeping out of the captain's way."

Captain Blade, the bravest buccaneer Sam had ever met, was terrified of parrots and only put up with this one because everyone pretended he was a crow — even though he was bright green.

"I'm on lookout," Sam told Crow, "and I can't see a thing with your beak in my face."

Crow flapped onto his shoulder and

nibbled his ear while Sam checked the view through his spyglass. This was the best place on the whole ship. He could see for miles across the sparkling blue ocean.

"Nothing to the right," he muttered. "I mean — on the starboard side." He swept his spyglass round. "Nothing ahead. Small island to port and I bet there's nothing behind . . . or should I say to stern . . . Wait a minute!" He focused the spyglass. The sun was gleaming off the sails of a large galleon on the horizon.

He leaned over the rail of the crow's nest. "Ship ahoy!" he yelled. "To stern. Under full sail."

He saw Captain Blade climb up to the poop deck and raise his own spyglass.

"British man-o'-war," he bellowed. "She's heading straight for us. Stash that treasure in the hold."

Sam watched the crew run to carry out the order, snatching up the bags of doubloons and disappearing below deck.

"We need more speed," cried the captain. "Hoist the top gallants!"

Fernando came speeding up the rigging to unfurl the sail at the very top of the main mast. He slid along the yard, the horizontal wooden pole just below the crow's nest, his nimble fingers pulling at the ropes to release the sail.

"Is that ship after our treasure?" shouted Sam over the slapping sound of the wind catching the sail.

"After us, more likely," Fernando shouted back. "As we're close to Jamaica, Governor Handasyde will have sent her. He's vowed to rid the seas of pirates."

"Are we going to fight?" asked Sam. He hadn't been in a full sea battle yet and he wasn't sure whether to be excited or scared.

"That man-o'-war will have twice as many guns as the *Sea Wolf*," replied Fernando. "And twice the crew."

Sam's mouth dropped open. "We don't stand a chance then."

"We do, my friend," said Fernando, releasing the last rope so that the top gallant swelled with wind. "We're much faster than they are. We'll outrun that scurvy ship. We have to." He looked up at Sam with troubled eyes. "If not, we'll be dancing the hempen jig."

Sam gasped with terror. He knew what that meant. It was how the pirates described being hanged on the gallows.

CHAPTER THREE

Sam gulped and stared at the man-o'-war. She looked terrifying with her towering masts and brilliant white sails.

He could hear Harry Hopp shouting orders for the crew to pull in the sheets – the ropes that controlled the sails – to make the best speed. Fernando sped down the rigging to obey. Soon the *Sea Wolf* was whipping through the waves.

Sam swept the sea with his spyglass to check that all was clear. As he scanned the island he caught a movement ahead. The bowsprit of a large vessel was appearing around the tip of the island in front of them. The *Sea Wolf* would have to adjust her course to avoid it. That could lose them time and they wanted to keep their lead on the man-o'-war.

"Ship off the port bow!" he called down.

Sam checked again and gave a shocked gasp. The ship was identical to the one that was following them. The dreaded Union Jack was flying from all her masts! And this vessel was swinging slowly round towards them, cutting off their escape. The *Sea Wolf* had been driven into a trap!

"It's another enemy ship!" he yelled at the top of his voice. "British man-o'-war!"

Fernando had said that they were outgunned and outmanned but Sam knew that now the pirates had no choice but to make a fight of it. It was a bit like being on the top board at the swimming pool – he felt eager to jump but scared at the same time.

"Loose the sails," Blade ordered the crew. "Man the guns!"

Sam felt the *Sea Wolf* slow as the sails lost the wind. He wished they could just speed away but the ship ahead would put a stop to that. He knew Captain Blade was going to need every fighter in his crew.

"Stay here, Crow," cried Sam, climbing out of the crow's nest.

He raced down the rigging, his heart thumping hard. The two men-o'-war were drawing close, one to port, the other to starboard, trapping the *Sea Wolf*.

He jumped to the deck, his heart thumping with terrified excitement.

Charlie ran up to him, her face pale but determined. "We may not have much chance," she muttered through gritted teeth as she handed him a cutlass, "but we'll give them a fierce fight!"

Fernando joined them. "Keep your weapons to hand, my friends," he said. "We'll need them if we're to beat these miserable scabs."

Sam felt his pulse steady. If he had to fight alongside anyone he couldn't wish for braver companions. Harry Hopp called them to fetch powder for the cannon. Sam put his cutlass in his belt and was down the hatchway to the gun deck and back with a keg of powder in seconds. But before the *Sea Wolf* guns were ready there was a deafening sound that sent shudders through the ship.

BOOM!

"They're firing from both sides!" gasped Charlie.

Smoke was rising from the enemy ports as the cannonballs screamed overhead.

"Return fire!" shouted the captain.

The cannon fuses were lit and soon it was hard to see through the dense smoke as the *Sea Wolf* guns roared in answer. But that didn't stop the enemy missiles. Most dropped harmlessly into the water, though some tore through the sails.

"Their aim is poor," grinned Fernando, dragging a sack of cannonballs across the deck.

"Lucky for us," agreed Sam. He thought it was strange that the sailors of a man-o'-war should be so careless, but he was too busy fetching gunpowder to worry about it.

Then, as suddenly as it had started, the firing stopped and there was an eerie silence.

The smoke on deck blew away and the two men-o'-war came into clear view. They were so close now that all Sam could see were their massive hulls looming over him from both sides. He gulped. It looked as if the *Sea Wolf* was a filling in a giant ship sandwich.

"Prepare to be boarded!" came Captain Blade's voice. Sam heard the sound of his crewmates' swords being drawn. He put down the powder keg and grasped his cutlass firmly. Charlie and Fernando stood next to him.

There were fierce shouts as the enemy sailors leapt onto the deck of the *Sea Wolf* from both sides and crossed swords with the pirate crew.

Sam and Charlie moved forwards to join the struggle but Fernando dragged them down the steps to the safety of the rope store. "There's something wrong here," he shouted above the noise of clashing swords.

"You're telling me!" gasped Sam. "Our crew are about to be captured and we're hiding below deck! Let's get up there! We've got the whole British navy attacking."

"Wait!" Charlie grasped Sam's sleeve to

keep him back. "Fernando's right. These men are not British sailors."

Sam peered out at the fierce fight. Now he could see that the enemy had no uniforms on, but were dressed in brightly coloured coats and loose breeches, and wore turbans on their heads. "Maybe they're in disguise," he suggested.

Fernando was shaking his head. "They don't fight like the British. And look at their weapons. Those curved swords are called scimitars. These men are corsairs."

Charlie gave a gasp of horror. "You mean pirates like us?"

Fernando nodded. "From the Mediterranean Sea. They must have stolen the British ships and got rid of the crew. They're known to be merciless."

"Then they don't want to take us prisoner." Charlie gripped her cutlass hard. "They'll kill us all!"

Chapter Four

Sam, Fernando and Charlie burst out of the storeroom, weapons flashing over their heads. With bloodcurdling cries they launched themselves into the fight. Sam was very grateful for the fencing lessons Charlie and the captain had given him. Without them, he'd have been cut to ribbons against these fierce corsairs. He thrust at the enemy and parried blows with his cutlass.

Captain Blade darted across the poop deck, his sword moving so quickly that it seemed invisible. Fernando was hanging from the rigging by one hand, kicking away the enemy and knocking them overboard. For a moment Sam couldn't see Charlie. Then he caught sight of the small figure expertly wielding her blade on the prow. She was fending off two attackers at once and beside her stood Sinbad, eyes burning, swiping at the legs of any corsair that dared to come near her. There was a flash of green and Crow came screeching down, claws outstretched. The brave parrot dive-bombed the invaders, sending them leaping over the side in terror.

A huge corsair suddenly came at Sam, swishing his scimitar evilly, and Sam forgot about everything but keeping the sharp steel away from his body.

He dived to the deck as the enemy fighter lunged at him. The man went stumbling past but another took his place, wielding a heavy stick. It came smashing down on Sam's wrist and his sword flew from his hand and spun across the wooden planks. He was helpless, with the point of an enemy cutlass at his throat. He caught the devilish glint in the corsair's eye. Sam knew that any minute now he would feel the blade go through him. He shut his eyes. Then there was a coarse yell and the fighting suddenly stopped. Everything was strangely quiet. Sam wondered if he was dead and hadn't felt the killer blow.

Cautiously he opened one eye. He seemed to be alive and he couldn't believe what he was seeing. His attacker had put up his sword and was swinging back to his own ship! The rest of the *Sea Wolf* crew were looking on, dumbfounded. Soon not a single corsair was left on the deck.

As the last man jumped on to the rail he turned to the *Sea Wolf* pirates. He wasn't wearing the flowing clothes and turban of a corsair like the others, but rough breeches and a bandana round his head. His face creased into a grin that was made more hideous by the three vivid scars in a line down his cheek. At the sight of the man's face Sam started in surprise. He'd seen the brute somewhere before – and he had a bad feeling about him.

"If you're thinking of following," the man snarled, "don't bother. You've got more important things to worry about." Then he leapt for his ship, shouted orders to his men and soon the two vessels had caught the wind and were off.

The pirates of the *Sea Wolf* stared at each other, stunned.

"I don't understand, Captain," muttered the first mate. "I thought we were done for."

"So did I, Harry," snapped the captain, picking his pistol up from where it had fallen. "They must have just wanted our gold."

Ben Hudson, the quartermaster, dived down the steps to the hold. He was soon back. "No, it's all there, Captain," he said in surprise. "Not a doubloon missing!"

"Now that *is* odd," said Harry Hopp. "It would have been a handsome haul."

"I'll tell you what else is odd," said Peter the cook. "They didn't even take my pies!" He pointed to a pile of squashed pastry on the poop deck. "They were fresh last Thursday. I left them out for lunch."

Sam tried not to laugh. The sight of Peter's pies were enough to make anybody run away.

"No one's dead, and they haven't taken our booty and we've not been captured," said Harry. "So what were those scurvy sea dogs doing here?"

"They've wasted our ammunition," called one of the crew.

"And our weapons," added another, holding up a bent cutlass.

"And given us a nasty wound or two," added a third, clutching his arm where blood was seeping through his sleeve.

"It must have been some stupid jape," growled Captain Blade through gritted teeth. "They were trying to make fools of us . . ."

"There's a fire!" shouted Fernando suddenly. "In the bows!"

Everyone turned to look. Smoke was billowing out from under the galley door.

Sam stared in horror. He knew how quickly fire could spread on a wooden ship.

"I don't understand," wailed Peter. "I put the cooking fire out the moment we saw the first man-o'-war."

"It was those dirty cowards!" cried the captain, shaking his fist at the distant enemy.

"I'll have them keelhauled! Fetch the buckets, men, before it reaches the gun deck."

"Get to it, lads!" cried Harry Hopp. "One spark on the gunpowder and we'll all be blown out of the water."

Sam could see that the crew knew the

fire drill. In an instant they were lowering wooden buckets on ropes over the side and pulling them up, full of sloshing water. Fernando crept cautiously to the galley door, flung it open and leapt aside as huge, crackling flames shot out.

Sam joined one of the chains of men, swiftly passing buckets from hand to hand. The captain and Harry Hopp were at the head of the lines, snatching the buckets and hurling the water onto the raging fire. The flames hissed but roared out again, threatening to creep up the foremast. The tar between the deck planks was bubbling in the heat.

And now the fire was licking along the bowsprit.

"Come on, men," bellowed the captain. "Double your efforts!"

Faces were grimy with black smoke and sweat but the pirates worked at top speed, determined to save their ship. The smoke choked them as they worked. Sam passed the buckets along as fast as he could, almost blinded by the soot in his eyes.

But at last the air began to clear and he could see that they'd won the fight. The flames fizzled and hissed and finally died.

The pirates stood together, catching their breath and gazing at the damage. The foredeck was a blackened ruin. It still smouldered, despite the dowsing of sea water. Above it rose the foremast, darkened by soot but still standing strong. The galley door was gone and inside there were a few charred pots and pans.

"My galley!" wailed Peter.

"As burnt as the food you give us!" chuckled Ned. "Look on the bright side, lads. We're still alive!"

"I was concerned for your leg, Harry," called Captain Blade, putting down his bucket. "One spark and it would have burned to a cinder, and then you'd have been Harry Hopping!"

The first mate grinned. "Aye, Captain. I'd have been Harry Hopping *mad!*"

"Look out, everyone," warned Ben Hudson suddenly. "Sinbad's on the prowl."

"By the look of him I'd say he's fought harder than any of us!" declared Ned, backing away.

Sinbad limped round the deck. His fur was more ragged than ever and one ear was bleeding. He wove through the crew without a single hiss, sniffing their feet and peering up at their faces. Sam knew who the surly ship's cat was looking for – his beloved Charlie. But why couldn't he find her? Sam's stomach gave a sickening lurch.

"Where's Charlie?" he cried, realising that she was nowhere to be seen.

The crew ran round the ship, searching from crow's nest to hold. At last they gathered again, shaking their heads.

Sam felt as if he'd had a bucket of icy seawater thrown over him. If she wasn't on the ship then there was only one explanation.

"Charlie's fallen overboard," he breathed in horror. "And she can't swim!"

CHAPTER FIVE

Sam dashed to the rail. Maybe Charlie had found something to cling to and was keeping herself afloat. But there was no sign of any movement in the water, just the gentle swell of the ocean. The others joined him, yelling her name and listening for a reply.

Sam realised that it was hopeless. The sea had swallowed her up.

Fernando put his arm round Sam's shoulders. "It's no good, my friend," he murmured. "A strong swimmer might manage to stay alive, but poor Charlie . . . She still hasn't learned a stroke."

"I should have saved her!" groaned Sam in despair. "I should have seen she was in trouble."

"You must not blame yourself." Captain Blade had come to stand with the two of them. "How could you have seen what was happening? We were fighting for our lives."

"And Charlie has lost hers." Sam's eyes pricked with tears.

"She was the bravest girl I've ever known," said Harry Hopp gruffly. "But our life is a hard one, Sam, and we have to get used to losing good shipmates."

The crew stood silently for a moment, heads bowed. Sinbad sat alone at the bows, watching the water forlornly. Sam decided

he'd throw his coin away when he got back
to the future. He never wanted to come
here again, not without Charlie.

It seemed so unfair after all she'd gone
through. She'd joined the crew to get away
from her evil stepfather. Sam thought
about the night he'd helped her escape —
and the vicious thug who'd nearly caught
them!

The image of the man with the scarred
face who'd led the corsairs suddenly

jumped into his
head.

"Just a minute!"
he cried, his
eyes lighting up.
"Charlie may not
have drowned at all!"

The others looked puzzled. "That's not
possible," Fernando murmured.

"We all mourn her loss, lad," said Ned,
"but you can't go thinking—"

"I'll explain," said Sam in excitement.
"We couldn't work out why the corsairs
attacked us, could we?"

"That's true," said Captain Blade. "They
left the *Sea Wolf* in a hurry even though
they had the upper hand in the fight."

"And they set a fire so we couldn't
follow," added Sam.

"Perhaps they hoped that the fire would
destroy the ship," put in Harry Hopp.
"Though it doesn't seem likely."

"It makes no sense at all," agreed the captain.

"By rights we should all have been down in Davy Jones' locker," said Ben Hudson.

"Us and the ship too," piped up Peter the cook, "if that fire had spread."

"We can't fathom it," said Harry Hopp, "so let's just say it was luck!"

"It wasn't luck at all," insisted Sam. "They did what they were paid to do. I know what they really came for. They were after Charlie!"

Ned squeezed Sam's arm. "Come and sit awhile," he said. "You're upset and your wits are muddled. Grief can do that."

Sam stood his ground. "I recognised one of the men who attacked us. He wasn't a corsair like the others. He was the man who was chasing Charlie when I rescued her. He's one of her stepfather's henchmen!"

Captain Blade frowned. "Surely her

stepfather would not send two ships full of fighting men to capture one young girl."

"Charlie's not just any young girl, Captain," answered Sam desperately. "If Eustace Gilbert gets hold of his stepdaughter, he'll make her sign all her wealth over to him. Then he'll be rich and Charlie will be dead."

Harry Hopp nodded. "Aye, lad, we know the story — and we know him to be a ruthless villain in need of money . . ."

". . . who would think nothing of sending an army of men to kidnap Charlie," added Fernando, "and set a fire to stop us following! I think you've found the answer, Sam."

"But are you *sure* that the man you saw was Charlie's pursuer?" asked Harry.

"As sure as I'm standing here," declared Sam. "He has three scars in a line down his cheek. They were fresh scratches when Charlie and I were escaping from

him, and they were bleeding heavily." He
nodded towards the ship's cat, who was
now draped miserably over the bowsprit.
"Sinbad gave them to him when he fought
him off."

"Hurrah for Sinbad!" called one of the
crew.

Fernando spun his knife in the air.
"He'd have suffered worse if I'd been
there!" he said fiercely.

"You might be right, Sam," said Harry Hopp. "If that was the plot it explains why they didn't take our treasure."

"Or my pies," said Peter.

"Exactly!" declared Sam. "I thought it was odd that their aim was so poor when they first attacked, but they have to deliver Charlie to her stepfather in one piece. She has to be alive to sign the new will."

Captain Blade pulled at the red braids entwined in his beard. At last he spoke. "I hardly dare hope it's true," he said, "but if Charlie is still alive, then by the heavens we will find her!"

CHAPTER SIX

"Set sail west!" ordered Captain Blade. "That's the way those bilge rats went."

Harry Hopp's stubbly face creased in a frown. "But we're still badly outnumbered, Captain. We can't take Charlie back by force."

"We certainly can't," said Blade fiercely. "We'll use cunning instead. We're not giving up on her. Jump to it!"

The crew raced to take up their positions and the sails filled with wind.

"Where do you think they're heading?" asked Sam.

"I'll warrant they're off towards Jamaica," said Blade. "They went in that direction."

"Jamaica?" Sam burst out. "Charlie's old home is in Jamaica!"

"So it is, by Zeus!" cried the captain, clapping Sam on the back. "Can you remember anything else, lad?"

Sam racked his brains.

"Jamaica's a big island," said Harry Hopp, scratching his bald head. "How will we know where they've gone?"

A name flashed into Sam's head. "Montego Bay!" he exclaimed. "Is that in Jamaica? I'm sure that's where she lived."

Captain Blade nodded and fetched a map from his cabin and laid it out on a barrel.

"Here's Jamaica," Sam quickly pointed

to a small island.
The old map made
it look like a turtle
swimming through
the Caribbean.

"Aye," replied
the captain. "And Montego Bay is in the
north. Just a few hours' sail if the wind
holds."

"Then we'll soon have Charlie back,"
said Sam eagerly.

"It won't be as simple as that, lad," said
Captain Blade. "Montego Bay is not a
place that welcomes pirates. We must
find a way to get into port without being
recognised."

Sam looked up at the snarling wolf head
and crossed bones fluttering from the
main mast. "Can we change our flag?"

"Aye," said the captain. "But the
figurehead will give us away as soon as
anyone spies it."

Sam knew he was right. The leaping wolf figurehead was famous throughout the Caribbean. It would be impossible to disguise it.

"Ship ahoy!" came a cry. "Off the starboard bow."

Captain Blade held his spyglass to his eye. "Merchant ship," he said, "and heading for Jamaica like us most likely. She's called the *Ocean Hero*."

"We'll be cutting across her path if we keep to this course," said Harry Hopp. "Any other day we'd be paying them a call and seeing what booty they'd like to share."

Sam watched the distant ship. *No one will stop the* Ocean Hero *sailing into Montego Bay,* he thought. And a fantastic idea bounced into his brain.

"Let's see if they'd like to share their ship!" he exclaimed.

"We don't want that old boat," said Harry Hopp. "We're *Sea Wolf* men!"

"I mean we borrow her," explained Sam. He turned eagerly to the captain. "We take that ship to Montego Bay. No one is going to be suspicious of a merchant ship going about her business."

Blade turned to Sam with an excited gleam in his eyes.

"By the full moon!" he roared. "That's an excellent plan, Sam."

"We'll be in Montego Bay before you can say albatross," said Harry Hopp.

The captain strode to the front of the poop deck and called to the crew. "Get ready for action, men. We're going to capture the *Ocean Hero*."

The crew of the *Ocean Hero* took one look at the fierce pirates and their leader with his belts full of weapons and surrendered immediately before scampering off to hide. Blade jumped across to the captured ship, while his men lashed her to the *Sea Wolf* with ropes. The merchant captain peeped out from behind a barrel.

"We haven't got any treasure," he quavered. "Go away!"

"And good morning to you, too," Blade said pleasantly, sweeping off his hat. "I have a bargain to discuss."

"What sort of bargain?" came the surprised reply from behind the barrel.

Sam could see that he'd been expecting to be killed in some horrible way.

"I wish to borrow your ship for a short while," Blade explained. "You and your crew will be guests on the *Sea Wolf* until we return."

The merchant sailors poked their heads out from their hiding places. They looked as if they could hardly believe their ears. But their captain decided that since he wasn't going to be run through he would show some bravado in front of his men. He stood up and squared his shoulders.

"And if we don't agree?" he asked.

"You would not want to find out what happens then," growled Fernando, showing the merchant captain the blade of his knife.

"But it would be quick," added Harry Hopp fiercely.

Sam smiled to himself. The worst the captain would do was make them walk the plank when they weren't too far from land. But the crew of the *Ocean Hero* didn't know that. They gulped and their captain turned pale.

"I agree to the bargain," he squeaked.

"I'll be needing your coat and hat, too," said Blade. "Mine are a little too conspicuous."

"Of course!" said the merchant captain, ripping his coat off and losing a few buttons in his haste. Captain Blade put them on. The coat strained across his broad shoulders.

"Now, please make your way to our vessel," said Harry Hopp, waving them on board. "Peter the cook will be pleased to serve you dinner."

The captives looked delighted at this news. Sam wished he was going to be there when they saw the food on offer. That would soon wipe the smiles from their faces.

Captain Blade and his rescue team
made the *Ocean Hero* ready to set sail for
Montego Bay.

"I leave the *Sea Wolf* in your command,
Harry," Blade called across the sea to the
first mate. "Look after her . . . and our
guests."

"Aye, aye, Captain," said Harry Hopp.
"And you bring that lass back. We miss her
something awful."

As the *Ocean Hero* pulled away there was
a scrabble of claws and Sinbad launched
himself from the *Sea Wolf* bowsprit, flew

across the gap and landed on the deck of the merchant ship. He ignored the crew and stalked to the front rail, staring purposefully ahead.

"On with the rescue!" yelled Captain Blade. "By thunder, we'll have Charlie back before daybreak."

CHAPTER SEVEN

Montego Bay was a busy port, with galleons, fishing boats and rowing skiffs weaving around each other as they came and went. The small town was surrounded by green forested hills. Along from the harbour, the sea washed up on golden sands. The afternoon sun shone brightly over a long headland with palm trees waving in the wind.

The *Ocean Hero* tacked into the middle of the harbour. Sam gripped the rail, waiting for an angry shout and the roar of a gun, but no one recognised the *Sea Wolf* crew. They were on a merchant ship so everyone thought they were merchant seamen. It was like when he'd gone to his Auntie Sarah's fancy-dress party as a giant cactus and no one had known it was him. It had been great until he'd popped all the balloons and stabbed his grandma in the bottom.

Fernando came to stand by him and they scanned each vessel in turn, trying to spot the men-o'-war.

"Supposing the corsairs have taken Charlie somewhere else," said Fernando, anxiously twisting one of his earrings. "We'll have no chance of finding her in time."

"Their ships have to be here," replied Sam, wishing he felt as sure as he sounded. "This is where she lived with her stepfather."

But he couldn't see the enemy ships among the many others that lay at anchor.

"Ahoy there, *Ocean Hero!*" came a shout.

A magnificent ship was approaching. It shone with fresh red and gold paint, and had the figurehead of a woman in an armoured helmet.

"It's the governor's ship!" hissed Ned.

The pirates gave each other worried looks. Sam felt sick. Had they made it this far only to be discovered and captured? That couldn't happen. Charlie was depending on them.

"Lie low, lads," muttered Captain Blade. "I'll do the talking."

The crew oozed into the shadows on the deck. Fernando and Sam squatted down, pretending to splice some ropes, their heads bowed. Captain Blade pulled his borrowed hat forwards so that the brim hid most of his face. He raised a hand in greeting to the man at the rail who was hailing them.

"How was your voyage?" called the sailor. "Any bad weather we need to know about?"

"Set fair all the way from Hispaniola," Blade called back.

"That's strange," said the governor's man looking intently at him. "I thought the *Hero* was coming from Cuba this voyage." He started to bring his spyglass up to his eye. Sam's breath caught in his throat. Any minute now he'd get a good look at Captain Blade, with the fierce braids in his beard and coat that was too small for him, and guess that this was not the crew of a merchant ship.

Blade shrugged helplessly. "That's what we thought too! Then the owner's wife gets a fancy for some French silk and we're sent off to Hispaniola because he likes to spoil her."

The man laughed, waved a farewell and walked back to his wheel.

Sam caught Fernando's eye. They grinned at each other in relief. That had been close.

"Drop anchor!" called the captain. "All eyes on the harbour. Those corsairs will be lurking somewhere."

Sam picked up his spyglass and scanned the water again. On the far side of the bay he picked out the shapes of two identical ships with tall masts and white sails. The Union Jack was flying from all the masts.

"There they are!" he cried.

The crew came to the rail.

"Aye, that's them all right," growled the captain. "I can see where we put a shot through one of the poop decks." He gave a laugh and pulled at his borrowed coat. "And they've copied my idea. One or two of the men have got naval uniforms on now. That'll keep the authorities off their tail."

Ned chuckled. "A corsair in a turban would stick out like a peg leg on a donkey."

Fernando's eyes narrowed as he ran his finger along the blade of his knife. "We should board them at once, Captain, and find Charlie."

"She won't be on the ship now, lad," said Blade, his hand on Fernando's shoulder.

"Then we've got to find out where she

is," Sam burst out. "She could be signing the will at this moment and then . . ."

"And we'll do that," Captain Blade assured him. "But we can't do it by force. We'll sneak on board and find a corsair who's willing to tell us where our shipmate is. Most rogues talk when they have cold steel at their throats. But we need darkness on our side for that. In the meantime, let's eat."

When the captain was out of earshot, Sam turned to Fernando. "I know the captain's right," he whispered, "but I can't bear to think of what may be happening to Charlie while we wait."

"She's brave," Fernando nodded. "But she's no match for her captors."

"I'm going to find her now," said Sam, through gritted teeth. "It looks like an easy swim."

"*You* are not going ashore," hissed Fernando fiercely. Sam glared at him.

Fernando grasped his hand firmly. "*We* are going ashore!"

Sam couldn't keep the beaming smile from spreading over his face. This mission would be much easier with two of them. "We'll be disobeying orders," he warned his friend.

"But we'll be rescuing Charlie," said Fernando, his eyes shining.

Sam peered over the rail at the shoreline. The sun was low over the headland now. "I reckon we've got time before the sun goes down. It'll give us enough light to see our way."

"Food up!" came a cry and they spun round to see Seth holding a steaming platter of fish. "Freshly caught!"

Sam's stomach rumbled. It smelt much better than anything Peter ever cooked. In fact, it reminded him of home when his parents started frying the fish and chips for the evening's customers.

"We should eat first," said Fernando, sniffing the air longingly. "It'll give us strength."

"Your stomach will have to wait," chuckled Sam. "We're going now while they're all busy!"

They slipped down to the deck below, squeezed through one of the gun holes and lowered themselves into the sea. The water was dark and cold, surprising Sam and making him gasp. He listened, hoping that no one had heard him.

"All's quiet," whispered Fernando. "Let's go."

Swimming with careful strokes so as not to make a splash, Sam and Fernando made for the shore. Fernando twisted onto his side, peering behind at the way they'd come.

"What are you looking at?" called Sam in a low voice.

Fernando turned back. He looked scared

in the shadowy light. "We have company!"
he croaked.

And now Sam could see it. A black fin,
cutting through the water and coming
straight for them!

Chapter Eight

Sam gulped. There was no way they could outswim a shark.

"Have you got your knife?" he cried.

Fernando was treading water beside him. "As always, but I don't want to use it," he said, his eyes fixed on the fin that was coming nearer and nearer.

"Of course not!" Sam knew that if they made the shark bleed, that would bring more sharks! "But we can't just stay here and wait to be eaten! Hang on a minute – I know what to do. I saw it on a TV programme . . ."

"What are you talking about?" snapped Fernando. "We are sitting targets here and you are gabbling nonsense!"

"I mean . . . my mum told me," said Sam, spluttering as he swallowed a mouthful of salt water. "Brave woman, my mum. Never got eaten by a shark. Knows what to do. 'Hit it, son,' she said."

"Where?" yelled Fernando.

Sam's brain whirred desperately. Was it in the eye or on the nose? "She didn't say."

They felt the water churn and the long sleek body of the shark was suddenly in front of them. Sam clenched his fists ready to strike.

As the shark loomed over him, Fernando struck out and punched it on the nose.

"Take that, you monster!"

The shark lurched and swam past. The water was calm again.

"I scared it off!" shouted Fernando in triumph.

"I don't think so," replied Sam. "Look, here it comes again."

This time the boys lashed out with their feet and fists. The shark slid by once more and disappeared.

"I bet it's getting ready for another attack," whispered Sam, anxiously scanning the water. Night was falling and it was getting harder to see.

"What do we do?" Fernando asked.

"Back to back," yelled Sam. "It could come from anywhere."

"Excellent idea!" Fernando trod water behind him. "I expect your mother told you that too."

Sam's eyes were stinging from the salt as he dipped his head under the water to see if he could make out the deadly attacker's approach.

Suddenly the water surged and the grey snout was almost upon him. He could see the huge mouth, with its rows of sharp teeth. *Oh, dear,* he thought. *I'm definitely on the menu.*

He kicked out hard, his trainer thumping into the side of the shark's gills. A shudder ran through the long grey body and it veered sharply away.

Sam scanned the water anxiously. Seconds passed but the shark didn't return. Was it waiting just below the surface, lulling them into a false sense of security? "Where is it?" he gasped.

"I've no idea," came Fernando's voice over his shoulder.

It was dark now. Sam felt sick. At any moment he might feel sharp teeth slicing into his leg . . .

"There!" cried Fernando, pointing to a triangular shape. "It's swimming away. We've defeated it, my friend!"

"I vote we don't wait for it to return with *its* friends," said Sam, heading for the shore with his fastest front crawl. He didn't care who heard him now. He wanted to be out of the water.

At last he could make out the gleam of the beach as the moon appeared from behind a cloud. His feet touched sand. Together, he and Fernando splashed through the waves and collapsed on the shore.

"I suggest we find a boat for the return trip," Sam gasped.

"Agreed!" said Fernando, holding out a hand to pull him to his feet.

Keeping low, they crept up the beach, making for the steps that led to the quay. A row of white houses stood in a ragged line along the quayside. Lights shone from a nearby tavern and they could hear deep voices singing and shouting.

"Which way?" asked Sam, shaking the cold water out of his eyes.

"I wish I knew," said Fernando. "I've

never been here before."

Sam racked his brains. Charlie had told them a little bit about her past life. Surely they could work it out. He thought of his computer game, *Daring Detective*, where you had to solve a crime by finding the right clues.

"What do we know?" he said.

Fernando's forehead creased in thought. "She told me that she lived in a big house looking down onto Montego Bay."

"Good," said Sam. "That sounds as if it's up the hill." He remembered Charlie telling him about her escape. She'd been very sad to leave her childhood home. "She said she had to escape from the back of the house," he told Fernando, "but it was sunset and it was lit up by the evening sun. She

was terrified that someone would see her."

"So the front of the house faces east over the bay," said Fernando. "That means it's on the western headland. But that's still a big area to search."

"Then we'd better get started," said Sam firmly. "Let's go."

A burst of song from the tavern floated out on the breeze as they slipped past.

"If only we could go in there and ask someone," said Sam. "But who could we trust? Anyone could be in the pay of her stepfather."

"We might end up with our throats cut!" nodded Fernando. "It's like finding a needle in a bundle of hay."

Sam felt itchy inside with frustration. This was getting urgent. Time could be running out for Charlie.

CHAPTER NINE

"Charlie must have said something else about her old home that can help us," said Sam desperately. "Think, Fernando."

"There was her nursemaid!" exclaimed Fernando.

"That's a great help," groaned Sam. "Her nursemaid isn't exactly going to be standing in the garden pointing the way!"

"Of course not," laughed his friend.

"But Charlie said she used to hide when her nursemaid was calling her to go to bed. She climbed out of her bedroom window and hid in the sea grape tree that grew at the front of the house. She was sad because she had a lovely garden and her stepfather let it go to ruin after her mother died."

"So we're looking for a big house, facing east with a messy garden and a sea grape tree," said Sam. "Well remembered, Fernando . . . but are you sure about the sea grapes? Don't they grow under the sea?"

"Of course not!" exclaimed Fernando, looking puzzled. "You must have seen them with their big round leaves. They're all over the Caribbean."

Whoops, thought Sam. *I should have known that.*

The wind had picked up now that night had fallen. It gusted against them and Sam

got a strong whiff
of sweets.

"Sugar!" he
hissed, making Fernando
jump. "I've just
remembered. Her
house was near a sugar
plantation called Merrily or Cherokee, no
... Verity! That was it. She could see the
building where they boiled the sugar from
her window. She said it always smelled
sweet. We just have to follow our noses."

"But the smell is all around us now," said
Fernando. "And there must be more than
one sugar plantation here."

Sam stretched out an arm and pointed
to a dirt road. "That way," he said
decisively.

"How can you be sure?" asked Fernando.

"A Silver can always follow his nose,"
said Sam solemnly. Fernando looked
impressed. "Actually there's a sign there,"

Sam admitted, pointing to a battered old piece of wood with 'Verity Plantation' written on it.

Fernando chuckled and ran off up the road. "You cheat," he called over his shoulder. "A *Silver* can follow me instead!"

The dirt road wound away over the hillside. It was hard going as there were deep cartwheel ruts that caught at their feet, making them trip. At each bend they could see the lights shining over the black water of the harbour. The smell of sugar was getting very strong.

"There," whispered Fernando, pointing to the shadowy outline of a large house. "That could be it. It faces east over the bay."

A wall ran around the boundary. There were gates at the front entrance but they were rusty and hanging off their hinges, so the boys were able to slip into the grounds easily. They followed the carriage tracks to the sprawling house. Sam looked up at the dark shuttered windows, heavy front door and the veranda that ran the length of the ground floor with a balcony above.

"This can't be the place," he murmured. "There's no tree for Charlie to have hidden in."

"Perhaps you're right," said Fernando. "We could try further up the road and . . .

Ai!" He cursed and hopped about rubbing his leg. "I walked into something hard."

Sam peered down among the overgrown plants at the edge of the veranda. "It's a tree trunk!" he exclaimed. "There was a tree here but it's been chopped down. I reckon it could be our sea grape!"

"Let's go and see if there's a way in round the back," said Fernando.

They crept round the house, feeling their way in the dark, stumbling through the overgrown shrubs.

"There's a broken window," hissed Sam.

He carefully put his hand through the hole in the pane and got his fingers round the catch. He eased it open.

"Follow me," he said, climbing over the sill.

The boys found themselves in a large room, lit only by the faint moonlight that filtered in through the window. A dirty cooking range stood against one wall and there were some cupboards beside it. In the middle of the room was a large wooden table.

"It's a kitchen," whispered Sam. He stood, listening. The house was so quiet that even his own breathing sounded loud. "Where do we start looking?"

To his surprise Fernando began to open cupboard doors and feel inside.

"What are you doing?" hissed Sam. "Someone will hear us. She's not going to be in there anyway!"

"But there might be food!" muttered his friend. "I'm so hungry, if I don't eat soon the growling in my stomach will give us away." He pulled out a chunk of bread and bit hungrily into it. "This is no more than a day old," he said, passing some to Sam. "Someone's been here recently."

"Then let's search the rest of the house," said Sam. He started to make his way round the table towards the door.

Suddenly they heard footsteps and the door was flung open so that it slammed against the wall. Sam and Fernando dived under the table.

Sam saw a man come in, carrying a lantern. He was dressed in rough clothes and had a brutish face. He began to prowl round the room. Sam and Fernando shrank back into the dark.

"You little thieves," he snarled, opening cupboards and shining the lantern inside.

"You won't escape me."

Sam and Fernando looked at each other in horror. Had they been discovered?

All at once there was a scraping sound and a flash of metal as the man snatched up a meat cleaver.

"I see you, you dirty little rascals!" he cried. He came straight at their hiding place, and raised the cleaver.

CHAPTER TEN

*C*rash! The cleaver smashed down on the table above their heads. There were terrified squeaks and the frantic scampering of tiny paws.

"I'll get you next time," cursed the man. "You see if I don't!"

"What are you doing, Ebenezer?" came an angry shout from another room.

The man stiffened as if afraid. "Rats in

the kitchen, Mr Gilbert," he gabbled. "I'm trying to get rid of them."

"Stop that and bring me some bread and cheese immediately!" came Eustace Gilbert's voice.

The man snatched up the bread from the cupboard and paused, holding it up to the light. Sam held his breath – he'd seen the bite marks! Sam hoped he wouldn't realise they were human! But the man just pulled away the edges where Fernando had bitten into the bread and slapped it on a plate with some cheese. "He can share it with the rats, him with his lordly, impatient ways," he muttered as he left the kitchen. "I wish I was his master, not his servant. Then I'd show him."

Fernando turned to Sam. "Well," he whispered, "we know that Eustace Gilbert is here."

"Then Charlie will be here too," Sam whispered back.

They scrambled out from their hiding place and crept towards the kitchen door. Sam eased it open and they peered out.

Short, sputtering candles on a table lit up a dingy square hall. Several rooms opened off it and from one they could hear a knife scraping on a plate.

"That's where Gilbert is," murmured Sam. "Let's check the other rooms."

They crept across the cold flagstones, Fernando holding his knife ready in his hand. Sam could see that this house had been really posh once, but now it was dirty and the paint was peeling off the walls. Without warning he walked straight into a huge spider web. He clamped a hand over his mouth to stop himself calling out in alarm. It must have been horrible for Charlie to be forced to live in this dilapidated house with her evil stepfather.

"Empty," he hissed, peering into a room and moving on to the next.

"You lazy good-for-nothing!" came Gilbert's voice. "Fill my glass. And don't take all night or I'll have you whipped."

"Shall I take some food up to the girl?" asked his servant.

"No!" roared Eustace Gilbert. "That would be a waste of a meal. The minute I've had my fill, I'll be up there forcing her to sign. She won't need food after that!"

Sam's blood ran cold. Fernando leapt forwards, his knife raised as if to attack, but Sam grabbed his arm.

"There's two of them," he hissed. "And they're grown men. We won't be any help to Charlie if we're dead."

Fernando reluctantly lowered his knife.

"Come on," said Sam firmly. "Gilbert said she's upstairs so that's where we're going."

Sam took a candle from the table and they tiptoed up the wooden staircase, flinching at every creaking step. The narrow landing ran round three sides of the first floor, overlooking the hall. The boys gently pushed open each door in turn, whispering Charlie's name. All the rooms were empty.

Fernando reached the last door. "It's locked," he said in a low voice.

Sam held up the candle. A heavy bolt was held firmly shut by a strong metal padlock.

"Charlie's got to be in there," said Sam. "We need to find the key."

Fernando shook his head. "We don't need a key."

"You can't kick the door in," Sam

 warned him. "That will bring Gilbert and his servant after us."

"Don't worry, my friend," murmured Fernando, slipping

his knife into his belt and fingering the padlock. "I have my ways." He removed a hooped earring, straightened it and bent over the padlock. "I haven't seen a lock like this," he muttered, poking the end of the earring into the keyhole.

"Can you do it?" asked Sam.

"I've never failed yet."

At last Sam heard a scrape and a clunk and the padlock was in Fernando's hands. Fernando slid the bolt across as silently as he could and pushed the door open.

Sam's flickering candlelight fell on a four poster bed with tattered drapes. A few girl's dresses lay in a heap on a chair. *This must have been Charlie's room,* thought Sam, gazing in horror as rats scuttled away to hide from the light. A small table stood in the centre of the room. A feathered quill pen and an inkwell had been placed beside a piece of parchment.

"Charlie?" Sam whispered.

He was answered by a muffled groan
from somewhere among the shadows.

"She's here!" cried Fernando, darting
into a murky corner. "Bring the light!"

Now Sam could see Charlie. Her
stepfather had left her in the dark. She was
tied to a chair, her eyes terrified and her
mouth tightly gagged. The candle flame
showed up black bruises on her swollen
face. Fernando wrenched at the gag, his
fingers struggling to undo the knots. At
last it came away. He threw it to the floor.

"What took you so long?" croaked Charlie, with a feeble smile.

"Sorry, your ladyship," said Sam, grinning. "We got held up by a fire."

"And a shark."

"And a man with a cleaver."

"Not forgetting the padlock!" said Fernando, slicing through Charlie's ropes. "I ruined a perfectly good earring to unlock that."

"I'm very grateful," said Charlie as Sam helped her to her feet.

"We have you now," said Fernando. "And we won't let that fiend hurt you any more."

"Very interesting," said a slimy voice. "And how exactly are you going to stop me?"

CHAPTER ELEVEN

Charlie was staring at the open door, a look of terror on her face. Sam and Fernando turned slowly. The shiny, round barrel of a pistol was pointing straight at Charlie's heart.

"Stepfather," she began. "Please don't—"

"Leave her alone," said Sam, stepping protectively in front of her as Eustace

Gilbert came into the room. He was a pale man with hollow cheeks and mean, narrow eyes. He wore a shabby black topcoat, with breeches tucked into ancient riding boots. He stared at them, a cold smile playing round his lips. Sam was suddenly reminded of the shark that had chased them.

Fernando's hand moved towards his knife.

Gilbert waved his pistol at him. "Drop that knife before I blow your brains out!"

Fernando scowled, but let his blade clatter to the wooden floor. It landed at Sam's foot. Perhaps if he was quick he could reach down and get it. However Charlie's stepfather seemed to have read his mind. Keeping the pistol aimed at them, he kicked the knife, sending it spinning away towards the wall.

"Now, Charlotte," he went on smoothly. "I'm going to shoot your friends. It's just a question of who goes first. You choose."

"No!" shouted Charlie, her fists clenched in fury. "Leave them alone. They're nothing to do with this."

Gilbert pointed the gun at Sam's head. "But I think they are, my dear. You see, if you sign the will and make your money over to me, I won't need to shoot them at all."

The life seemed to go out of Charlie. Her head fell to her chest. "Then I have no choice," she said brokenly. She stumbled towards the table and picked up the quill.

"Don't do it, Charlie," said Sam, starting forwards.

"Careful, boy," warned Gilbert nastily. "My finger could easily slip on this trigger."

Charlie picked up the quill and peered into the inkwell. "There's no ink," she said with a frown.

"Don't play the fool, girl," snapped Eustace Gilbert. "Sign your name at once."

Charlie stuck the quill into the stone pot and wiggled it about.

Gilbert stared suspiciously at her.

"See!" she declared, trying to write her name. The nib scratched at the document, leaving no mark. "I can't sign without ink. You need to fetch some more."

"If this is a trick . . ." growled her stepfather, snatching up the inkwell.

Quick as a flash, Charlie stabbed the quill point deep into the back of his hand.

Gilbert gave a shriek of pain and the pot went flying, splattering the room with black ink.

Before Charlie could move, Gilbert grasped her viciously round the throat. The blood from his hand dripped onto her shirt.

"Run for your lives, boys!" she shouted.

But Gilbert had already aimed the gun at them. "They're not going anywhere!" he snapped.

Sam felt sick. This looked hopeless. Or was it? Charlie had managed to catch Gilbert off guard so perhaps he could do the same. He had to distract him. He put his hands up. "I've had enough of this," he said. "I'm not hanging around to get shot on account of some girl." He turned to Fernando and gave him a quick wink. "You coming, Fernando, or are you going to argue with me *as usual*?" Sam could see that Fernando had grasped his meaning.

"You're a lily-livered coward," he retorted, gritting his teeth fiercely.

"No one calls me a lily-livered coward!" shouted Sam, leaping on his friend and knocking him to the ground. They rolled over and over, pretending to punch each other.

"A sea sponge has more guts!" cried Fernando.

"I'd rather be a gutless sea sponge than a scurvy scoundrel!" puffed Sam, grabbing Fernando round the throat and looking as if he was throttling him.

Fernando made choking sounds and thrashed his arms about.

"Stop that!" yelled Gilbert, pointing the pistol at one and then the other in panic. "I'll shoot!"

"You keep out of this, Mr Gilbert," panted Sam, scrabbling to his feet and circling Fernando, teeth bared. "This is between me and this prattling porpoise here!" He'd heard Harry Hopp call someone that and he'd been dying to try it out.

"Prattling porpoise?" screamed Fernando, snatching up the heavy inkwell from the floor. "I'll beat you to a pulp for that."

His eyes were flashing and for a millisecond Sam wondered if he really *was* going to going to get beaten to a pulp.

Fernando raised the inkwell as if to throw it at him. Then his arm swung

through the air and suddenly the stone pot was flying across the room. Gilbert had no time to duck. It smacked him squarely on the forehead with a sickening *thud*. He toppled to the floor like a fallen tree. Quick as a flash, Charlie snatched up his gun and trained it on him.

"He's out cold," she said, rubbing her neck where his hands had been.

"We've got to get out of here." Sam crept to the door and listened. "That servant must have heard the noise." He peered into the dark corridor. "All clear," he hissed.

Fernando found his knife and blew out the candle. "He left you in the dark, Charlie. Let's see how he likes it." They tiptoed into the corridor. Fernando slid the bolt home and rammed the padlock back into place. "And if he manages to find the door, he won't be able to get out."

"Oi, there!" a shout came from the

gloomy hall below. The servant came running up the stairs, waving a ladle.

Charlie instantly pointed the gun at him. "Did you want something?" she asked sweetly.

The man took one look at the pistol, dropped the ladle and scampered back to the kitchen, slamming the door behind him. The three friends piled down the stairs and out onto the carriage track in the front garden.

Charlie flung her arms round both boys. "Thank you. I owe you my life."

"*And* you owe me an earring," laughed Fernando.

"Let's get back to the ship," urged Sam, looking round. "I won't feel safe till we're back on board."

But before they could move, tall figures loomed out of the shadows. They raised their scimitars with a swish, blocking the way to the gates. Their leader was a man that Sam recognised — a man with three livid scars in a line down his cheek. He held up a lantern.

"Looks like the girl's escaping, lads," said the man, turning to the grim-faced corsairs behind him. "And that won't do. Mr Gilbert won't have any money to pay us with until she's dead." He snapped his fingers. "Take them!"

In seconds the three friends were caught, hands wrenched behind their backs and weapons snatched from them.

Sam thought quickly. "Eustace Gilbert will never pay you," he told them. "We heard him talking. He's going to keep Charlotte's money for himself."

"That's right," Charlie added. "He's nothing but a lying hornswoggler."

Fernando strained against his captors. "If you let us go, our captain will reward you in gold doubloons!"

"Good one, Fernando," muttered Sam

as the man looked from one to the other. "Scarface is thinking about it."

But at that moment the shutter above clattered open and Eustace Gilbert appeared on the balcony, swaying dizzily.

"Bring the girl back here!" he ordered. "I'll double your reward once she's dead."

"Don't listen to him!" shouted Charlie.

Scarface strode over and looked up at the balcony. "They're saying you won't pay us."

Gilbert gave a derisive laugh. "And you believe three stupid children?"

"Their captain's going to give us gold," Scarface went on defiantly.

"You only have to take us down to the harbour and you'll get what you're owed," said Sam. That was true. Captain Blade would give them a fitting reward – but he was sure it wouldn't be gold.

"They'd say anything to save their scrawny necks," sneered Eustace Gilbert.

Scarface scratched his head. "You agree to triple the money and we'll bring them straight to you," he called up to Gilbert.

"Agreed."

The corsairs cheered and waved their swords.

"Just the girl," Charlie's stepfather went on. "I don't need the boys. You can kill them where they stand."

CHAPTER TWELVE

"No!" shrieked Charlie as Scarface dragged her towards the house.

Sam and Fernando found themselves surrounded by a circle of corsairs, their scimitars raised.

The friends looked at each other in despair. There was no way out this time.

"Avast there!" came a rousing cry from the gates. "Men of the *Sea Wolf* — attack!"

The corsairs spun round. Captain Blade, his face grim, was charging along the carriage track. Ned, Seth and the others were close behind. With a clash of swords the pirates threw themselves at the enemy.

Sam's knees wanted to wobble with relief but he knew there was no time. He snatched up a fallen branch and swung it at the legs of the corsairs, toppling them like ninepins. Fernando was already hurling stones at them.

Sam heard a cry nearby. It was Charlie, kicking and thrashing in Scarface's grasp.

Sam rushed to help her. But at that moment a harsh yowl filled the air.

Scarface stopped in his tracks, his eyes full of terror.

Sam grinned to himself. *Charlie doesn't need my help,* he thought.

A mangy black cat, hackles raised and spitting like a demon, was standing in Scarface's path. And from the look on the man's face, he hadn't forgotten the ship's cat.

Sinbad pounced, claws outstretched. Scarface gave a whimper, dropped Charlie and ran as fast as he could towards the dark garden. The cat was after him in an instant. Distant hisses and yelps could be heard as Sinbad chased him through the undergrowth.

A fallen scimitar spun at Sam's feet. He grasped the handle and raised the heavy blade.

"I'll have that," said Charlie, a wild grin on her face. "I'm the expert!"

Sam handed it over and swung his stick around his head instead. "Go, Charlie!" he yelled at the top of his voice and threw himself into the fight.

Now the pirate crew formed a terrifying line. Fernando, Charlie and Sam were shoulder to shoulder, beating the enemy back towards the gates.

As soon as the corsairs saw the road beyond, they turned and fled.

"Come back you cowards!" screamed Eustace Gilbert from the balcony.

Captain Blade put up his sword and stormed towards the house, his face like thunder. "You're the bigger coward, you vile sea weevil!" he called up to Gilbert. "Getting others to do your dirty work."

"I'll get even with you," snarled Charlie's stepfather. "She'll sign one day and then the money will be mine. You wait."

"By Mars," roared the captain, "if you ever come near that maid again, you'll wish you'd never been born!"

Gilbert disappeared in a trice.

"To the port, men," ordered Captain Blade. "We'll not tarry in Montego Bay a moment longer."

Charlie turned towards the garden. "Puss!" she cried. "Puss, puss." A black streak of fur flew through the air and into her arms. Charlie stroked Sinbad under the chin, took one last look at her old home and then marched towards the gates.

With Sinbad clinging round her neck, Charlie was first to swing aboard the *Sea Wolf* when the *Ocean Hero* sailed up alongside. Repairs to the *Sea Wolf*'s galley had already started but the pirates threw down their tools with a cheer and ran to greet their crewmates.

"I cannot believe I'm safely home," Charlie sighed, scratching Sinbad between his tattered ears. The mangy cat slid down into her arms, purring loudly.

"Who's a brave boy?" she cooed, stroking the cat's belly. "You saw off that nasty man, didn't you?" She grinned happily. "You wouldn't think he could hurt a fly!"

The crew cringed as Sinbad gave them an evil glare.

Charlie looked up at the pirates, her eyes

shining. "Thank you, everyone," she said. "You're all heroes."

Ned shuffled his feet in embarrassment. "Well, I'll swing to the moon on an anchor chain," he said. "We were glad to do it." A broad smile spread over his face. "You should have seen us, lads," he told those members of the crew who had stayed with the *Sea Wolf*. "The minute we found that Sam and Fernando had gone, we were after them."

Seth took up the tale. "The captain sneaked onto one of the men-o'-war and he soon found out where Charlie had been taken."

"We knew that's where the boys would be heading," added Ned.

"And they turned up just in time," Sam added. "When I saw the captain charging along to rescue us—"

"Belay this talk," said Captain Blade, good-naturedly. "We should be setting sail. Where are our guests, Harry?"

The crew of the *Ocean Hero* shuffled onto the deck from below. They all looked rather pale in the lantern light.

"We are most grateful to you for the loan of your ship," Blade told their captain. "But I'm sure you'd like to be off now."

"Could we not thank them first, Captain?" said Fernando mischievously. "They could join us for some breakfast before they go. I'm sure we have some porridge that's only a month old . . ."

But the crew of the *Ocean Hero* turned green and their captain clutched his stomach. He waved a hand feebly at Blade. "No!" he cried in horror. "We've had quite enough food." And, with that, he and his men ran to the side of the ship and were gone, back to the *Ocean Hero*, in an instant.

"Set sail for Skeleton Island," ordered Captain Blade, standing at the rail and looking up at the stars.

"You'd better make yourselves scarce," Ned whispered to the boys. "The captain won't have forgotten that you jumped ship."

Sam and Fernando gulped. Keeping low, they crept towards the hatchway to the gun deck.

"Not so fast, you boys!" bellowed Blade, his gaze still fixed on the dark skies. "In my cabin, now!"

CHAPTER THIRTEEN

"He must have eyes in the back of his head!" hissed Sam as the boys mooched along to the captain's cabin.

The moment the door was shut behind them, Blade began to roar. "How dare you go ashore without permission? I will not have a disobedient crew on this ship!"

"Sorry, sir," muttered Sam. "It was just that we couldn't wait—"

"You went against my orders and you must take your punishment."

"We had to help Charlie," Fernando pleaded.

Blade glared at them, drumming his fingers on the table.

"Coming aboard!" came a squawk at the open porthole. Crow landed on the sill and peered in at them.

Captain Blade froze as the parrot flew in and began to strut up and down the table. "Yo ho ho," said Crow cheerfully.

"Get it out of here," croaked Blade.

"But, Captain," said Sam innocently. "You were just going to tell us about our punishment . . ."

"Take that bird away and I'll forget all about it," said the captain, beads of sweat on his brow.

Sam gave Fernando a grin and coaxed Crow onto his finger. The boys charged out of the cabin before Blade could change his mind.

"Did you train Crow to do that?" asked Fernando, impressed.

"No," laughed Sam, as they threw themselves down next to Charlie on the poop deck. "But he has perfect timing!"

"Perfect timing," repeated the parrot.

"You two seem very happy with your punishment," said Charlie, puzzled.

"Crow persuaded the captain to let us off!" chuckled Fernando.

The *Sea Wolf* was whipping through the water under a bright, starry sky. The crew were singing a jolly shanty as they worked.

This is the life, thought Sam.

But all of a sudden his fingers and toes began to tingle. The magic doubloon was about to whiz him back to the twenty-first century. He had to hide before he vanished

in front of the entire crew. He leapt to his feet.

Charlie realised what was happening. "Off to your mother's?" she said quickly.

Sam nodded. "See you soon."

He jumped off the poop deck and threw himself behind a barrel. At once he felt himself sucked into the dark, whirling tunnel. He landed with a bump on his bedroom floor, on top of his best clothes.

"Sam!" came his mother's voice. "I hope you've made yourself smart. Arnold's here."

Sam pulled on his best shirt and trousers. They were completely crumpled after being landed on by a time traveller. Arnold would take one look at him and go on and on about the history of ironing! If only Crow could pop up to get him out of it!

But Sam wasn't a brave buccaneer for nothing. If he could face cut-throat corsairs, he could cope with boring cousins.

And while Arnold droned on, Sam would just think about his next amazing *Sea Wolf* adventure!

CREW MANIFEST

Sinbad

Crow

Thomas Blade
Captain

Peter Craddock
Ship's Cook

Fernando
Rigger

Don't miss the next exciting adventure in the
Sam Silver: Undercover Pirate series

THE DEADLY TRAP

Available in January 2013!
Read on for a special preview
of the first chapter.

Chapter One

"Take that, you villain!" yelled Sam Silver, stabbing viciously at his reflection with a ruler.

He fought his imaginary enemy over his duvet and round a chair and trapped him in the wardrobe. His super sword skill had saved the day! But then, he'd had lessons from experts – a bunch of fierce Caribbean pirates.

It sounded impossible. His home in Backwater Bay was thousands of miles from the Caribbean and the pirate crew of the *Sea Wolf* had lived three hundred years ago. But Sam had an amazing magic coin to take him there whenever he wanted.

Sam had never forgotten the day he'd found the gold doubloon in a bottle washed up on the beach. It had been sent to him by a pirate ancestor of his, Joseph Silver. When he spat on it and rubbed it, it whisked him back in time to the *Sea Wolf* and its crew of brave buccaneers. The coin was his most prized possession and he kept it in its bottle on a shelf in his bedroom.

Sam swished his ruler wildly in the air, knocking the bottle flying. It hit the lampshade, bounced off his pillow and landed on the floor at his feet. He snatched it up and checked for cracks.

No, it seemed to be OK, but the cork was
missing and the coin that should have been
inside had gone.

"Disaster!" he cried, scrabbling about
on the floor, searching for the precious
doubloon.

There was no sign of it. Shining
his torch under the bed, he could see
something glinting near the wall. He fished
it out with a coat hanger. It was only a
lump of silver foil. He feverishly searched
his bin in case the coin had fallen into it.
He found a sock, two apple cores and a

squashed sandwich, but no gold doubloon. This was serious. The magic coin seemed to have vanished into thin air! Without it Sam couldn't travel back to the *Sea Wolf*. He gulped at the idea of never seeing his friends, Charlie and Fernando, and the pirate crew ever again.

"Sam!" His mum was calling from their fish and chip shop below the flat. "Can you pop to the supermarket for me? We need some milk."

Sam groaned. How could he concentrate on buying milk when he'd lost his magic doubloon? But he knew he'd be in trouble if he didn't go.

He kept glancing round the room as he slipped his left foot into his trainer.

"Ow!" There was something hard in there. He pulled his foot out and tipped the trainer upside down. The doubloon tumbled out onto the carpet.

Sam snatched it up and held it tightly

in his hands. That had been the worst moment of his life. Then he had a dreadful thought. Supposing the coin had lost its power now he'd dropped it. He'd better check it out. Then he'd go to the shops for his mum. That was the great thing about the magic doubloon. However long his pirate adventure lasted, he knew it would bring him back to exactly the same time in the present – if it still worked.

He pulled on the tatty jeans and T-shirt that he always wore when he went time travelling, and rammed on his trainers. Then he spat on the coin and rubbed it on his sleeve. At once his bedroom whooshed around him in a mad spin. He felt himself being sucked up as if he was in a giant vacuum cleaner.

Sam landed with a thump on the floor of a small wooden storeroom. He could hear the timbers creaking and feel the room swaying. Awesome! He was back on the *Sea Wolf*.

The shouts of the busy crew came from the main deck above. Sam jumped up. His pirate jerkin, belt and neckerchief were on a barrel, along with his spyglass. Charlie always put them there for him. She was the only one who knew he was a time traveller. Everyone else believed he popped home now and then to see his mum, which was true, of course. He just had a longer journey than they realised.

Stowing his coin safely in his jeans pocket, he threw on his pirate clothes and grabbed his spyglass. He ran up the stairway, bursting out onto the bright, sunlit deck. The blue ocean sparkled, the patched sails were tight in the wind and the flag with its snarling wolf's head and crossed bones fluttered merrily at the top of the mast.

Someone had hung some washing on a line strung across the deck. Patched shirts and breeches flapped in the breeze.

I didn't know pirates had washday! thought
Sam. *Hope I don't have to do the ironing!* He
ducked under the line of clothes to find
the crew and cannoned straight into
someone coming the other way.

"Sorry," he gasped. "I was—" He
stopped. He was looking up into a
face he'd never seen before. What had
happened? He was on the right
ship, but where was the
Sea Wolf crew?

Find out how the adventures began in . . .

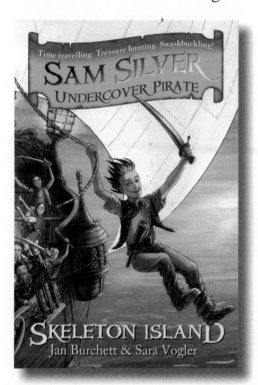

Join Sam Silver aboard the pirate ship,
Sea Wolf, for a rip-roaring adventure
on the high seas! Can Sam lead the crew
to buried treasure, or will he be forced
to walk the plank?